COUNTING TO CHRISTMAS

NANCY TAFURI

COUNTING TO CHRISTMAS

SCHOLASTIC PRESS · NEW YORK

Published by Scholastic Press, a division of Scholastic Inc., *Publishers since 1920.*

SCHOLASTIC and SCHOLASTIC PRESS and associated logos are trademarks and/or registered trademarks of

Scholastic Inc. No part of this publication may be reproduced, or stored in a retrieval system, or transmitted in

any form or by any means, electronic, mechanical, photocopying, recording, or otherwise, without written

permission of the publisher. For information regarding permissions, write to Scholastic Inc.,

Attention: Permissions Department, 555 Broadway, New York, NY 10012.

Library of Congress Cataloging-in-Publication Data

Tafuri, Nancy.

Counting to Christmas / Nancy Tafuri. — 1st ed.   p.   cm.

Summary: A child counts the days to Christmas, from one to twenty-five,

preparing a surprise for the woodland animals as she waits.

ISBN 0-590-27143-1.

[1. Christmas decorations — Fiction. 2. Christmas — Fiction. 3. Animals — Fiction. 4. Counting.]

I. Title.   PZ7.T117Co   1998   [E] — dc21   97-32059   CIP   AC

2   4   6   8   10   9   7   5   3   1

8   9/9   0/0   01   02   03

The illustrations for this book were created using watercolors and ink.

The text is set in 56-point Giovanni Book

Book design by Nancy Tafuri and David Saylor

Printed in Singapore   46

FIRST EDITION, OCTOBER 1998

For Cristina

I'm counting
to Christmas!

Days 1, 2, and 3
I paint, cut,
and paste.

Days 4 and 5
I write,
stamp,
and send.

Days 6, 7, and 8
I pour, measure, and mix.

Days 9, 10, and 11
I shape, bake,
and decorate.

Days 12 and 13
I wrap and tie.

Days 14 and 15
I pop and string.

Days 16, 17, and 18

I sing and play.

Days 19 and 20
I cut, spread,
and sprinkle.

Days 21, 22, and 23
I trim and gaze.

Day 24 I share,

and give,

and wait.

Day 25!
Merry Christmas!

With Love and Joy
to All!

COUNTING TO CHRISTMAS CRAFTS

YULETIDE CARDS

✦ red paper ✦ gold or yellow paper ✦ star-shaped cookie cutter or cardboard stencil ✦
✦ pencil ✦ white glue or paste ✦ envelopes ✦ markers, glitter pens, or colored pencils ✦

Cut out a rectangle of red paper and fold in half. Be sure that it will fit into the envelope. Trace a star onto the gold or yellow paper, and cut out. Paste the star on the front of the card. Write a holiday message inside with the glitter pen, markers, or colored pencils.

POPCORN-CRANBERRY GARLAND

✦ about 10 cups plain popped popcorn *(if air-popped, let it sit out overnight)* ✦
✦ 1 package raw cranberries ✦ carpet thread ✦ blunt carpet needle ✦

Ask a grown-up to help. Double-thread the needle by passing 5 to 6 feet of thread through the needle and knotting the two ends together. Alternate popcorn and cranberries, pushing them to the end of the string as you go. Make one long garland by tying shorter garlands together. Florist's wire can also be used instead of needle and thread.

Spicy Gingerbread Cookies

FOR COOKIES:

✦ 3 cups flour ✦ $\frac{1}{4}$ tsp. salt ✦ 1 tsp. baking soda ✦ 2 tsp. ground ginger ✦

✦ 1 tsp. ground cinnamon ✦ $\frac{1}{2}$ tsp. grated nutmeg ✦ $\frac{1}{4}$ tsp. ground cloves ✦

✦ $\frac{3}{4}$ cup dark brown sugar ✦ 12 Tbs. unsalted butter ✦ $\frac{1}{2}$ cup molasses ✦ 1 egg ✦

FOR DECORATIONS:

✦ 3 egg whites ✦ 4 cups confectioners' sugar ✦

✦ an assortment of raisins, candied cherries, and candies such as red hots and gumdrops ✦

Ask a grown-up to help. In a medium bowl, whisk together the flour, salt, baking soda, and spices. In a mixing bowl, blender, or food processor, cream together the brown sugar and butter until fluffy. Add molasses and egg and beat until blended. Gradually beat in the flour mixture till well-blended. Press the dough together to form a thick, flat disk. Wrap in plastic and refrigerate for at least two hours.

Set the oven to 350° and grease a baking sheet. Using a floured rolling pin, roll the dough out on a floured surface until $\frac{1}{4}$-inch thick. Use cookie cutters to cut out shapes. Make a hole $\frac{1}{2}$-inch from the top if you want to hang the cookies on the tree. Use a spatula to move the shapes to the baking sheet.

Bake cookies 8 to 10 minutes. Bottoms of cookies should be lightly browned. Transfer the cookies to wire racks, allow to cool, and make icing as follows.

Royal Icing: In a large mixing bowl, blender, or food processor, beat egg whites and sugar together until smooth. For colored icing, add a few drops of food coloring and mix till the color is even. For painting, thin the icing with water; to thicken, add more sugar. For piping, you may use pastry bags or small plastic bags with a tiny hole cut in the corner. Use icing as glue for the candy decorations.

Makes approximately 36 5-inch-by-3-inch cookies.

Outdoor Animal Treats

✦ ribbon or string ✦ pinecones ✦ peanut butter ✦ birdseed ✦
✦ apples ✦ oranges ✦

Pinecones: Pour birdseed into a shallow bowl. Tie a doubled piece of ribbon around the top of a pinecone. Be sure the ribbon is long enough to be placed around the branch of a tree. Coat the pinecone with peanut butter using a butter knife. Roll the pinecone in the birdseed. Place pinecone decorations in a bowl and refrigerate till you are ready to hang them outside.

Fruit treats: Ask a grown-up to help you cut the apples and oranges in half lengthwise. Tie ribbon around the middle and knot tightly at the top. Secure with a long pin if necessary. Use the rest of the ribbon to make a large loop for hanging.